SPID
THE SPIDER
GOES TO THE MOON

WRITTEN BY JOHN EATON ILLUSTRATED BY MELISSA SHEPHARD

Spid the Spider Goes to the Moon

First published as a paperback in 2022.

ISBN 978-199-9669-8-74

Published by Spidling Productions Ltd
Meadow Court, Minehead Road, Taunton, Somerset, TA2 6NS, England
Copyright © 2022 by John Eaton. All rights reserved.

British Library Cataloguing in Publication Data

A catalogue reference for this book is available from the British Library.

Printed and bound in Great Britain by Biddles Ltd, King's Lynn, Norfolk

This book is printed on acid-free paper responsibly manufactured from sustainable forestry in which at least
two trees are planted for each one used in paper production.

Website: www.spidthespider.com
Email: spid@spidthespider.com
Facebook: www.facebook.com/spidthespider
Instagram: www.instagram.com/spidthespider
Twitter: www.twitter.com/spidthespider
YouTube: www.youtube.com/spidthespider

With grateful thanks to my wife Sue, Darren Cullum, Peter Dymond,
Melissa Shephard, Michael Smetham, Alexa Tewkesbury,
Guy Tomlinson, Alistair Whiteley and Alexa Whitten.

And especially to my granddaughter Evaleigh,
without whom, Spid would not exist.

Additional illustrations by Yuliya Vasina and final composition by Chrissie Venn.

THIS BOOK FEATURES:

MR CHEEZY FEET

HERMAN

SPID THE SPIDER

SPID'S GIRLFRIEND BID

QUEENIE

HELLO SPIDLINGS!

Spid the spider here. I live in a village called Spider Webdon, which has its own steam train station. I can go almost anywhere when it's open. It's spidtastic.

The bus service is rubbish though and there are no buses at all on Spundays.

My house is at the top of a hill. I live there on my own and I work *very* hard for *very* little pay. Which isn't helpful when you're trying to improve your prospects.

I like listening to music called SpidRap and I've got a girlfriend called Bid. One day, I'd like to marry Bid – *if* I ever earn enough money to get married.

I do try hard to be good. I want to be a better spidling. But sometimes … well … let's just say I get a bit carried away. That's when Bid has to put me straight. She's clever at that.

And did I mention I write songs? I've written some about the adventures I have in my books. I sing them too. If you have a listen, you can join in and sing along …

Spid had had a hard day.

"I've had such a hard day," he moaned. "Work, work, work, then work some more. It's all I ever do. No wonder I've got back ache and leg ache and arm ache. If I had a neck, I'd probably have neck ache too."

To ease his aches, he decided to have a shower. "And then, Spid," he said to himself, "you must have a soothing cup of Earl Moth tea. You know that always makes you feel better."

The shower and the tea did make Spid feel much more cheerful. Especially when he realised he could now settle down for the evening and read his book.

"Excellent idea, Spid. Emm, emm ..." he said to himself.

Spid was reading a book by H. G. Spids. It was called *The First Spidling on the Moon* and, funnily enough, it was about the first spidling on the moon. If you didn't realise a spidling *had* been to the moon, then it's high time you read H. G. Spids' book.

Spid loved stories about space.

He loved science fiction TV series too, like *Spidlings in Space* and *Spid Trek*. He even loved songs with a bit of a space theme. "Spidlife on Mars" by Spidvid Blowy was one of his favourites.

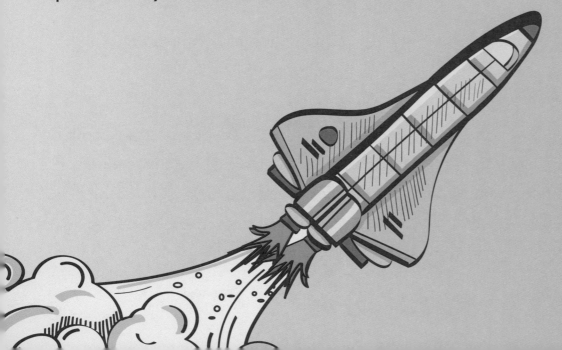

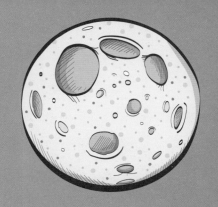

Not that Spid wanted to go to Mars. It was too far away. And he wasn't sure how he felt about visiting a planet named after a chocolate bar. His girlfriend Bid said the chocolate bar was named after the planet but Spid didn't believe her.

4

They've called it "Planet Mars" for a reason, he thought. I wouldn't chance it. Supposing I got there and found myself knee-deep in nougat?

But the moon ... How Spid dreamed of going to the moon! It was so much closer. He could get on a flight, land there, walk about a bit and be back in time for tea.

He'd once mentioned this to his friend, Herman, but Herman had looked doubtful.

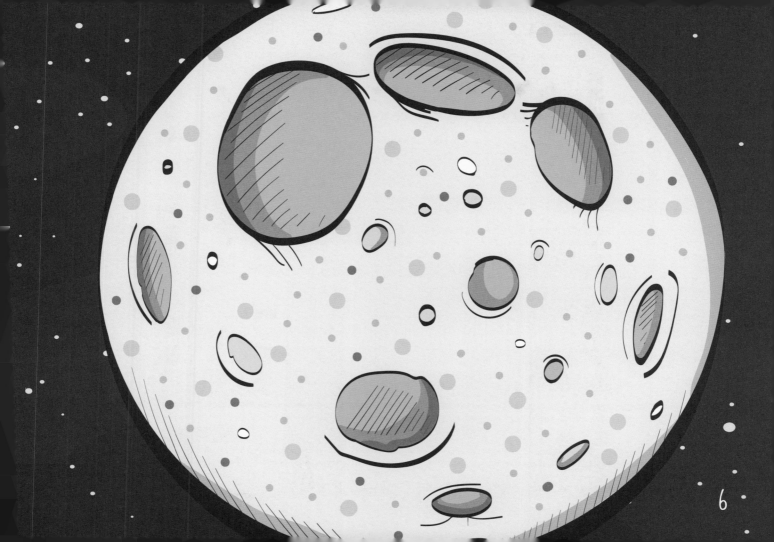

"I think you might need to take your tea with you," he'd said. "And definitely a flask of something hot. The first men who went to the moon took one hundred hours just to get there. After the seventy-seventh, they probably wished they'd stayed at home and mowed the lawn instead."

Spid couldn't imagine anyone wanting to stay at home to mow the lawn if they had a chance to go to the moon. Even if it did take one hundred hours to get there.

"Ah, well," he said to himself. "It doesn't matter how long it takes to get there, you'll never be able to go, Spid. You couldn't afford it. If you can't afford to get married, you *definitely* can't afford to go to the moon. Which is a shame," he added. "All that cheese. Emm, emm ..."

Bid had told Spid the moon wasn't made of cheese but, once again, he didn't believe her. After all, if she was wrong about a chocolate bar being named after the planet Mars, she could easily be wrong about the moon too.

I wonder if any spidlings will ever go to the moon again, Spid thought to himself. Apparently, there's a moonster up there. He looks down on Spiddle Earth and is very angry with everyone. They say he's best left there on his own ...

9

Just as Spid was thinking this, Bid called in to see him.

"We really need to get on and book a holiday," she said. "Our last one didn't end well, what with that nasty old pandemic. I think we deserve a treat. But we'll have to get a move on if we're going to get one of the cheap deals."

Spid wasn't sure. "The trouble is, Bid," he said, "even going on a cheap holiday costs money. And money's something I haven't got a lot of. If I'm going to spend money going somewhere, I'd rather it was somewhere I really want to go. Like the moon."

"The *moon?*" Bid looked surprised. "You've never mentioned wanting to go to the moon before."

"Maybe I haven't," said Spid. "But right now, that's the only place I do want to go. That would be a real adventure. I'd like an adventure."

He paused and shook his head wistfully. "Just an impossible dream, though. Even if there was a way to get to the moon, it would be far too expensive for a spidling like me. If I can't afford to get married, I *definitely* can't afford to go to the moon."

"I see," said Bid. "Well, funnily enough, I think I might have found the very thing. Sir Richard Branston Pickle has just set up a brand-new service to the moon. And guess what? There are some spaces left."

12

"Spaces left?" Spid's eyes opened wide. "On a flight to the moon?"

"Oh, yes," replied Bid. "Apparently, Sir Richard is finding it hard to fill the flight because the toilet is on the outside. So he's giving a huge discount."

Spid didn't like the sound of the outside toilet but he did like the sound of going to the moon. He liked it a lot.

"Well, let's book, then," he said. And he skipped excitedly round his kitchen table. "I can't believe it. We're going to the moon. We're actually *going to the moon!*"

"We actually are," replied Bid. "Perhaps Herman would like to go to the moon too. I'll ask him."

Spid grinned. "I hope there's free Spider Cider up there," he said. "Imagine me drinking Spider Cider on the moon. That'll be worth a selfie."

When Bid rang Herman, he said, yes, please, he'd very much like to go to the moon.

"Although I don't much like the sound of the outside toilet," he added. "But I suppose I'll have to manage. If I need to go, perhaps I'll be able to hold it till we get there."

So Bid sat down with Spid's computer and opened the Worldwide Spider Web to book their trip. Just in time too. She managed to get the last three places on Sir Richard Branston Pickle's moon rocket.

Spid was thrilled. He was also thrilled to be able to leave all the arrangements to someone else. If he could have an adventure without having to lift one of his many fingers, so much the better.

"I wonder if it smells cheesy up in space?" he said, and he sniffed thoughtfully.

Bid gave him a hard stare. "You do know, Spid," she said, "that the moon isn't made of cheese?"

"It might be," Spid replied. "We'll find out when we get there."

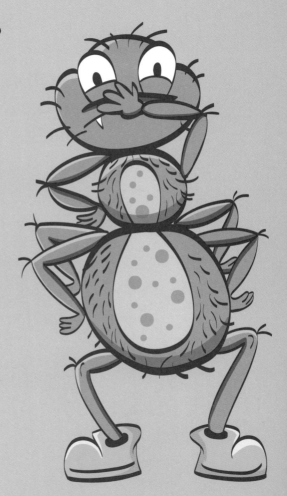

17

The next evening, Spid and Bid visited Herman to talk about their trip.

"They say the moon's made of cheese," said Herman.

Bid sighed. "You and Spid spend far too much time together," she said. "The moon *isn't* made of cheese."

"But what if it is?" Herman went on. "How did the cheese get there?"

"Well ..." said Spid in quite a grand-sounding way.

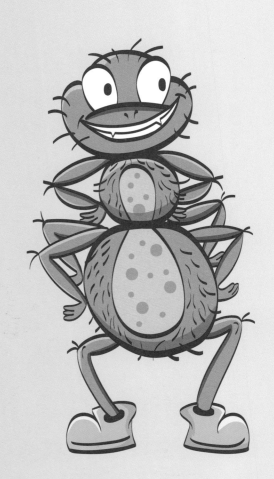

Bid rolled her eyes upwards. She knew what was coming. Whenever Spid said, "Well …" in quite a grand-sounding way like that, it meant he was about to tell a very long story. A story that wasn't at all likely to be true.

"One day," Spid went on, "Farmer Spid O'Spid decided to go to the market to buy a new calf. But the calf he bought wouldn't eat grass. She'd only eat waspburgers and French flies and drink Arachno-Cola.

"'Perhaps,' said the farmer, 'her rather *unusual* diet will give her milk a rather *unusual* flavour. And perhaps,' he added, 'I shall become famous for her *unusual*-tasting milk all over Spiddle Earth.'

22

"As it turned out, the only unusual thing that happened was that the calf grew up to be ginormous."

"How ginormous?" asked Herman.

"As ginormous as an elephant," replied Spid. "Only bigger."

"Bigger than an elephant?" Bid looked doubtful. "I've never seen a cow bigger than an elephant."

"Ah, yes," said Spid. "But have you ever seen a cow that would only drink Arachno-Cola and eat waspburgers and French flies?"

"Well ... no," Bid had to admit.

24

"Exactly," said Spid. "Now, Farmer Spid O'Spid called his cow Queenie," he went on. "By the time Queenie was the size of a large mountain, there weren't enough waspburgers and French flies around to fill her ginormous tummy. So the farmer told her she'd have to eat some grass as well.

"The problem was that Queenie then ate *all* the grass. So there was none left for the other cows. And they faded away and were never seen again."

"What – never?" said Herman.

"Never," said Spid.

Herman looked rather sad.

26

Spid didn't want him to dwell on the fading cows, so he hurried on. "Anyway, because Queenie ate all the grass, she ended up making *lots* of milk. Gallons and gallons and *gallons* of it. So much, in fact, that the local spidlings couldn't possibly drink it all."

"So what happened to it?" asked Herman.

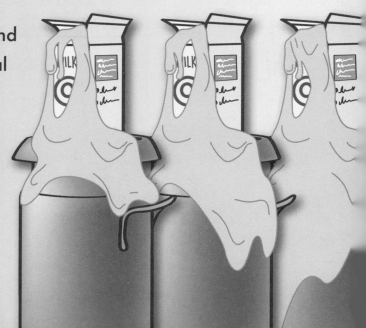

"I'm getting to that," replied Spid. "Farmer Spid O'Spid turned it into cheese. An especially scrummy sort of cheese called Lymespid."

Bid folded her arms and gave Spid one of her stern looks. "You don't seriously expect us to believe this nonsense, do you?" said Bid.

Spid shrugged. At least, he shrugged as much as he could, given that he didn't really have any shoulders. "I'm just telling you the story," he said.

Herman frowned. "If there was all that milk," he said, "there must have been a lot of cheese."

"There was." Spid nodded. "Lymespid cheese covered every field. And Farmer Spid O'Spid sold it and made a fortune. Until, one day ..." He paused dramatically.

Herman was almost afraid to ask. "Until one day ... what?"

"Queenie had eaten all the grass, of course. And without any grass to eat, she stopped making milk. And without any milk, Farmer Spid O'Spid couldn't make cheese. So the cheese disappeared."

"But …" Herman looked as though he might cry. His bottom lip quivered. "But without any grass, and without enough waspburgers and French flies, what will happen to poor Queenie?"

"Now, now, don't upset yourself, Herman,"
said Bid.

Bid was starting to worry. When Herman got cross,
he got smelly. And it took AGES for the smell to go
away. But sometimes, he also smelt bad if something
made him sad. Right at this moment, Herman looked
very sad indeed.

Bid glared at Spid. "This story has a happy ending – *doesn't it, Spid*?" she said. And she glared harder.

"Well, it certainly has an ending," Spid replied. He ignored Bid's hard glare. "You see, Farmer Spid O'Spid had an idea.

"He and the other spidlings built a giant catapult. They would catapult Queenie to the moon. While she was up there, the grass on Spiddle Earth would have a chance to grow again. Then, when there was enough of it, they could fetch her back.

33

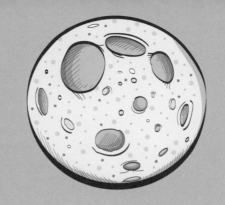
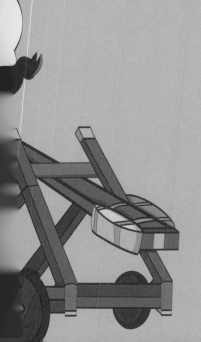

34

"So that's what they did. One day, when the catapult was ready, they sat Queenie on it and twanged her up to the moon. And there she stayed."

Herman wanted to ask what there was for Queenie to eat on the moon. But he didn't get the chance.

"The spidlings wrote a song about it, you know," Spid pressed on. "It's called 'Queenie'. Would you like to hear it?"

"No," said Bid. "Just finish the story, please, so we can go home."

Spid shrugged again, without any shoulders. "Well, Farmer Spid O'Spid soon started to miss all the money he'd been making from selling his cheese," he continued.

"Then one night, he noticed something. For the very first time. The moon was *covered in cheese*. Lymespid cheese. The soft yellow cheese with a yellow rind that he used to make. Emm, emm. Licketty-lips ... That's what gave the moon its soft yellowy glow. Also quite nice under foot, I should imagine," Spid added. "Creamy but very walkable."

Herman was starting to get impatient. "But what happened to Queenie?"

37

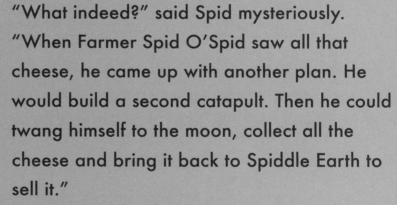

"What indeed?" said Spid mysteriously. "When Farmer Spid O'Spid saw all that cheese, he came up with another plan. He would build a second catapult. Then he could twang himself to the moon, collect all the cheese and bring it back to Spiddle Earth to sell it."

"And did he do that, Spid?" Herman asked. He listened with wide eyes.

Spid cleared his throat. He'd been talking so much it had got rather dry. "Ahhuum … The answer is yes – and no.

"Farmer Spid O'Spid catapulted himself to the moon. There, he found more cheese than he knew what to do with. The trouble was that he hadn't thought about how he'd get back to Spiddle Earth. So, once he was there, he had to stay.

"And the longer he was there, the more covered in cheese he became.

39

40

"That's why spidlings now call him 'Mr Cheezy Feet'. And he is the moonster."

If Herman's eyes had opened any wider, they would have popped out of his head. "So there really is a moonster on the moon?"

"Oh, yes," Spid said. "He's been up there ever since. In fact, if you look up when the moon is full, you can see him waving his arms and being very angry."

"Ooh," said Herman. "I wonder if Mr Cheezy Feet smells when he gets angry, like I do?"

"I think he smells all the time, Herman," answered Spid. "Of cheese."

Bid had had enough. "If I were you, Herman, I'd take all this with a huge pinch of salt. Spid's obviously made the whole thing up."

"You can believe it or not," said Spid. "But I'll take you both to meet Mr Cheezy Feet when we get to the moon. And that's a promise."

42

"By the way," said Herman, "what happened to Queenie?"

"Ah," Spid replied. "I'm afraid she passed a long time ago. But, don't be sad, Herman. Because for a mountain-sized cow with a mountain-sized appetite, she had a wonderful life. I mean, how many mountain-sized cows do you know of who get to go to the moon?"

Herman could only agree that he didn't know of any.

43

The day of the moon trip finally arrived.

Herman the harvestman was quite nervous. He'd flown in an aeroplane before. But that was very different to being blasted into outer space. Especially in a flimsy-looking rocket that looked like a toothpaste tube.

As Spid, Bid and Herman took their seats in the space rocket, Spid was – well – over the moon. He could barely stop his legs from jiggling with joy.

Then the engines started ... **_BOOOOM!_**

And the countdown began ... 5, 4, 3, 2, 1 - **BLAAASSTT**
... and the rocket lifted off.

It flew one thousand miles every minute.
That meant that in two hundred and fifty
minutes, they would be on the moon.

There was no point explaining
this to Spid, of course. Maths
just gave him a headache.

Besides, as they rocketed into the sky, Spid didn't care how fast they were going. In fact, he felt so relaxed, he fell asleep. Bid only woke him when they were about to land.

"Ha! Here already!" chirped Spid.

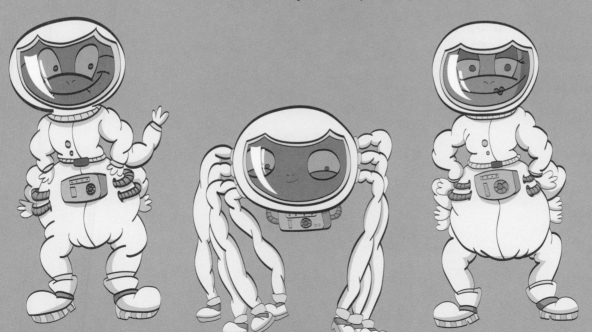

Bid sorted out their spacesuits. Herman's was a large suit. Spid's was a bit smaller. Bid's was a bit smaller than that. And they were all a bright white with blue trimmings.

When they had managed to climb into them, Spid looked at Bid. "You should wear bright white with blue trimmings more often," he said. "You look very nice."

Bid couldn't help blushing. She waited until Spid wasn't looking. Then she put on a little more lipstick so that the bright white with blue trimmings would make her look even nicer.

48

When they got off the rocket, a moon buggy was waiting for them. Bid had arranged it.

"So we can get around and see the sights," she said.

"See the sights?" said Spid. "What, cheese, cheese and more cheese? Because it's all cheese up here – old Lymespid. I'll drive, shall I?"

49

Herman didn't get the chance to ask, "Actually, would you mind if I drive?"

And Bid didn't get the chance to say, "Spid, the moon isn't made of cheese."

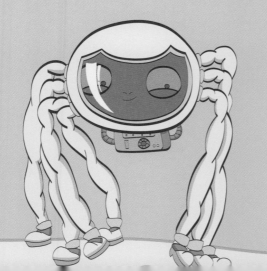

Because Spid had already leapt into the driver's seat and started the engine.

50

Bid and Herman had to leap quickly into the buggy too or he might have driven off without them.

"Let's go and see the moonster – Mr Cheezy Feet," Spid went on. "I've told you how angry he is. How every full moon, he shouts and waves his arms at us on Spiddle Earth. Well, it's a full moon right now!"

With that, Spid typed "cheezy moonster's hideaway" into the spidnav, and off they went.

As it turned out, Spid didn't need directions from the spidnav. Mr Cheezy Feet was shaking his fists at Spiddle Earth and shouting and ranting very loudly. All Spid had to do was follow the grumpy noise.

When they found him, Spid, Bid and Herman stared. Mr Cheezy Feet was a very odd sight indeed. He was so covered in cheese, they'd never seen anything like him.

52

Bid's mouth dropped wide open. She couldn't stop it. Mr Cheezy Feet, the moonster, was real after all.

"**EXCUSE ME**," shouted Spid. He'd decided not to park the moon buggy too close to such a grumpy moonster. This meant he had to shout to make himself heard over Mr Cheezy Feet's shouting.

"*I SAID, EXCUSE ME!*" Spid shouted louder.

54

Mr Cheezy Feet turned. He was very surprised to see a moon buggy with three spidlings sitting in it. So he stopped his own shouting straightaway.

"I don't know why you're shouting at Spiddle Earth and waving your arms about like that," Spid went on, still shouting. "No one can hear you down there, even though you're very loud up here."

"There's no need to shout," said Mr Cheezy Feet. "I may be covered in cheese but there's nothing wrong with my ears."

Herman looked puzzled. "If you don't mind my asking, Mr Cheezy Feet," he began, "why are you so angry?"

Mr Cheezy Feet looked even angrier. "I'm angry," he replied, "because I've been up here forever. No one's been to visit me and no one has helped me get off the moon."

56

Spid thought for a moment. "The thing is, Mr Cheezy Feet," he said, "back on Spiddle Earth, we all know the story. We know you went to the moon to bring back all the cheese because you wanted to make lots of money. And we know you were so eager to bring back the cheese that you didn't think about what you'd need to get home again.

"So really," Spid added, "this is your own fault. You were being greedy and you didn't plan. You put your *greed* before your *need*, so to speak."

He glanced round at Bid and Herman, looking pleased with himself. "Greed before your need – good, eh? Emm, emm ..."

Bid didn't answer. Her mouth was still wide open at the sight of the moonster.

"That sounds about right to me," agreed Herman. "You've been on the moon, for many moons, because you didn't make a proper plan. And that's not Spiddle Earth's fault."

"It most certainly isn't," said Spid. "I'm afraid it's *your* fault, Mr Cheezy Feet. So it really is no good blaming anyone else."

Mr Cheezy Feet looked thoughtful, in his own cheesy kind of way. "I suppose you're right," he said. "I never thought of it like that. I should have catapulted a catapult up here first. Then I could have catapulted myself back." He sighed. "But I was too greedy for cheese and because of that, I'll never see my home again."

Mr Cheezy Feet looked sad now as well as thoughtful. And with a quick "thank you" and "goodbye", he trudged back to his hovel.

"That's sorted that, then," said Spid. "I don't expect we'll see him shouting and waving his arms about every full moon anymore."

Bid beamed at him. "Spid, you're so clever," she said. "You always said there was a moonster. You always said the moon was made of cheese – and you were right!"

"I knew you were right all along," Herman said. "And now you've helped Mr Cheezy Feet understand that he can't keep blaming other spidlings for his own mistakes. It's time he took responsibility for them himself."

"Yes." Spid nodded. "Yes, I suppose I have."

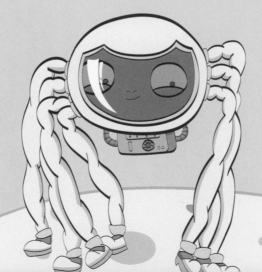

"It's at times like this," Bid said, "that I'm very proud to be your girlfriend, Spid."

To show just how proud she was, she put on some more lipstick.

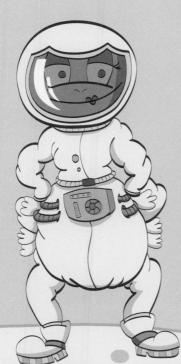

When she'd finished, she said, "I just wonder, though ..."

"What?" asked Spid.

"Well, Mr Cheezy Feet has learnt his lesson now. And he's been up on the moon for a very long time."

"Yes?" said Spid.

"Do you suppose that Sir Richard Branston Pickle would let him fly back to Spiddle Earth with us – so that he could go home?"

Spid looked doubtful. "I don't know about that," he said. "There would be a very cheesy smell in the rocket."

"Not necessarily," said Bid. "What if Mr Cheezy Feet travelled home in the outside toilet?"

Spid thought for a moment. That was actually quite a good idea. "But what if anyone *needs* the toilet?" he asked.

"Not a problem," said Herman. "They can all do what I did on the way here."

"And what's that?" asked Spid.

Herman grinned. "They can hold it till they get home."

Spid had an idea too. He could sing to the other passengers all the way back. Whether they wanted him to or not. That would keep their minds off the moonster in the outside toilet ...

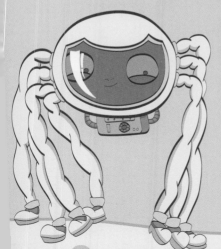

THE CHEESE SONG (MR CHEEZY FEET)

Mr Cheezy Feet, sitting on the moon.
That's why I'll sing this song in tune.
He knows a lot about cheese,
'Cos that's his expertise.

Milk and cheese, he was at ease with.
It's the only thing that he agrees with.
Though he Camembert to be a Gouda,
Like he thinks he could and should have.

He knows his way around a board of cheese,
From his Beaufort to his finest Bries.
Delights in his fine, strong Gruyere,
Partial to some soft fromage frais.

Mr Cheezy Feet, sitting on the moon.
That's why I'll sing this song in tune.
He knows a lot about cheese,
'Cos that's his expertise.

Once he even tried to show me
How to cover a mascarpone.
But he couldn't sip an Arachno-Cola
When swallowing a slice of Gorgonzola.

He would really like to Roquefort,
As his Feta is now in the dock store.
If he wants to get it back,
He'll have to speak to Monterey Jack.

He likes his cheese in his cottage
With a side dish of liquid pottage,
Served from a recipe by Nigella,
With an extra helping of shredded mozzarella.

His earthly home is in Wensleydale, really,
Where he samples his cheese Caerphilly.
But if he wants to eat something better,
There's nothing like a Somerset cheddar.

Mr Cheezy Feet, sitting on the moon.
That's why I'll sing this song in tune.
He knows a lot about cheese,
'Cos that's his expertise.

68

QUEENIE

Hey, spiddle spiddle,
The farmer had a giggle,
'Cos the cow was catapulted over the moon.
The cow was so big, she tripped over a twig.
As a result, we won't be seeing her anytime
soon.

Queenie, we love your milk,
With the texture of well-warmed silk,
And the comfort of a southern highland kilt,
And the snugness of an old bedding quilt.

But the milk changed to cheese,
Making other cows ill at ease.
Lymespid cheese in the morning breeze,
With the evening scent of honeybees.

Hey, spiddle spiddle,
The farmer had a giggle,
'Cos the cow was catapulted over the moon.
The cow was so big, she tripped over a twig.
As a result, we won't be seeing her anytime
soon.

But the milk brimmed over
From Dunbar to Dover.
No more roaming in the clover,
Too much cheese, even for a grocer.

69

So, we sent you to the moon,
Catapulted in mid-late June.
And that's why we sing this tune
on this balmy afternoon.

Hey, spiddle spiddle,
The farmer had a giggle,
'Cos the cow was catapulted over the moon.
The cow was so big, she tripped over a twig.
As a result, we won't be seeing her anytime
soon.

It was a one-way ticket ride
To a world on the other side,
Where you will now reside
To make your cheese with pride.
Queenie, we loved your cheese,
And your milk in our teas.
Every time, you tried to please –
On that we can agree.

Hey, spiddle spiddle,
The farmer had a giggle,
'Cos the cow was catapulted over the moon.
The cow was so big, she tripped over a twig.
As a result, we won't be seeing her anytime
soon.

SPID
THE SPIDER

You can listen to these songs on Spid's website and on his album, *We're Having Fun*. They are also available from all good music stores.

Spid the spider returns in *Spid the Spider Visits the Seven Wonders of the World.*